OAK PARK PUBLIC LIBRARY

31132 012 496 422

DEC - - 2012

OAK PARK PUBLIC LIBRARY
ADELE H. MAZE BRANCH

W9-ASR-881

For Victoria,
the world's best
mummy!
Giles
x

For Kate,
with love
Emma
x

Text © 2010 by Giles Andreae
Illustrations © 2010 by Emma Dodd
First published under the title I love my mummy in
Great Britain in 2010 by Orchard Books, an imprint
of Hachette Children's Books.

All rights reserved. Published by Disney • Hyperion
Books, an imprint of Disney Book Group. No part
of this book may be reproduced or transmitted in
any form or by any means, electronic or mechanical,
including photocopying, recording, or by any
information storage and retrieval system, without
written permission from the publisher. For
information address Disney • Hyperion Books,
114 Fifth Avenue, New York, New York 10011-5690.

First US edition, 2011
10 9 8 7 6 5 4 3 2 1
R969-8180-0-10319
Printed in China
ISBN 978-1-4231-4327-7
Reinforced binding

Library of Congress Cataloging-in-Publication Data
on file.

Visit www.hyperionbooksforchildren.com

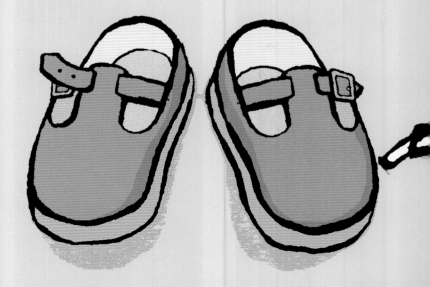

I love my mommy

Giles Andreae & Emma Dodd

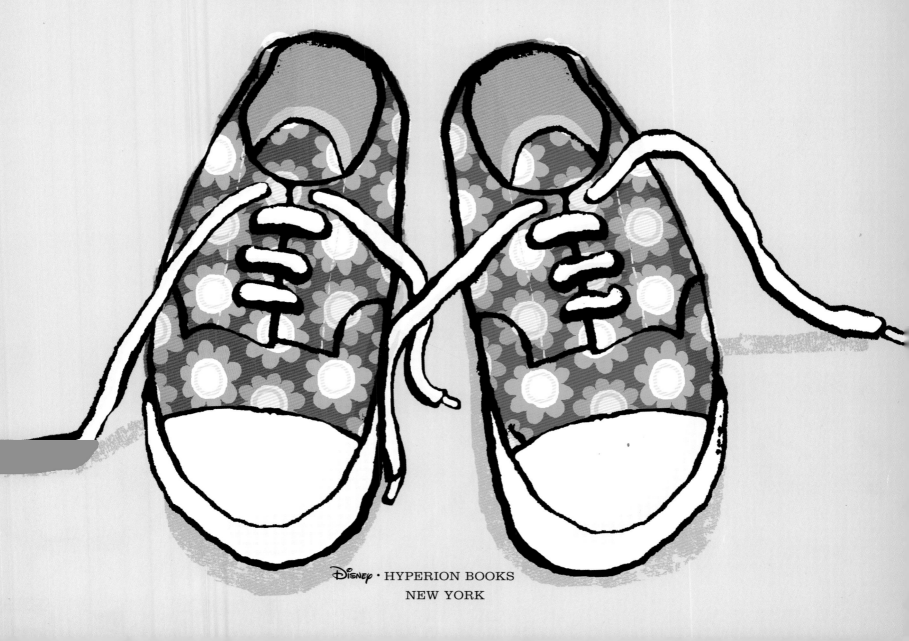

DISNEY • HYPERION BOOKS
NEW YORK

I love my mommy very much,

She's great to cuddle, soft to touch.

I like to watch her brush her hair,

And dance around in her underwear!

She helps me wipe my grubby nose,

And tickles me between my toes!

And even when I start to cry,

She wipes my tears until they're dry.

She takes me shopping in the car,

And sings my favorite songs, by far.

She holds my hand

when we go out,

And asks me not to scream and shout.

She cooks me yummy things to eat,

And when I'm good I get a treat!

She's really very kind to me,

She even helps me learn to pee!

We love to giggle in the bath,

Splashing bubbles makes me laugh.

She likes to kiss me on the head,

And read me stories in her bed.

I know that if you met her, you . . .

. . . would really love my mommy too!